Praise for 'The Secret

'A super book for kids ⸺ ⸺ᴜᴋᴇ. I loved reading this book with my daughter who adored it, and we can't wait for the next one.'

Alex Brown – Best Selling Author

'A perceptive and purrrrfect story, for young cat lovers, that makes you paws (!) for thought about why your cat is behaving as it is. Great fun!'

Samantha Tonge – Best Selling Author

'WONDERFUL BOOK! Funny and charming I found it such a good read. Naughty cat lets you take a walk in your felines paws. My 4 year old really loved this book too, it made her laugh often and kept her interested until the last word. So much so that she has now claimed said book and I need to buy another copy for myself! Looking forward to reading Naughty cats future books'

Dawn – Amazon Reviewer

'A lovely little book written with cheeky charm and a great sense of fun. The writers observation of cats made me chuckle out loud! Clearly written by a true cat lover. Highly recommended.'

Rebecca – Amazon Reviewer

'Lovely book thoroughly enjoyed by my children aged 5 and 9. They laughed throughout and are now ready for us to get our own naughty cat!'

Miss E Meyrick – Amazon Reviewer

'Such a good idea! From the perspective of our feline friends! Such a good read and ring true for my furry friends!'

Kate – Amazon Reviewer

'A very funny book, a must for the young readers.'

Kathy – Amazon Reviewer

'What a brilliantly written book by Daniel Riding. Many have said it is great for youngsters, I agree wholeheartedly but I have been through a bit of a tough couple of weeks and needed a pep up and this has been absolutely PURRRRFECT for me, as a new kitten growing into an adolescent cat owner, I have watched my fur baby Winston so much closer and looked at his play and wondered if he really does all these things! My tears of grief turned to tears of laughter and I thank you Daniel Riding for that and for me to be able to read my Kitty more. I have also passed the link to my friends to buy and their children have loved it. So for adults and children alike a beautiful look into the world of. Naughty Cat.

I do hope there will be more and it becomes a series.'

'Loved this book. Great for kids and adults alike. Can't wait for the next instalment.'

'Wowweeee what a joyful and mischievous book to read. I absolutely loved it and had me chuckling along with it being written as if it's the cat. Pure brilliance for kids or fun-loving adults too.'

'Now I am the first to admit I am probably classified as a 'mad cat lady' I have always been owned by felines! So this book immediately grabbed my attention. While The Secret Diary of a Naughty Cat is classified as a children's book it is a pleasure for any age group. Have you ever wondered what your cat is thinking? The reasons behind their zany antics or the pure aloofness that some animals maintain. Well look no further, this story enlightens you in the most fantastic way. I loved the excellent observations the author has made on his own fur babies. It is spot on and written with humour and love. Short snappy chapters highlight the various eating, sleeping, pooping, playing patterns and make us humans understand that we are in fact only here for the cat's pleasure! A Wonderful debut and I look forward to reading further entertaining cat adventures from Daniel.'

Ali – The Dragon Slayer

'Naughty Cat is an utter delight! It is full of mischief, humour and charm. It is obvious that the author is a cat "parent" and that he understands his pets very well. Great for all ages and I am looking forward to more of these diaries! A wonderful debut!!'

TishyLou – Tishylou's Book Page

'I was sent this delightful little book for review and I can honestly say I loved it. The individual chapters discuss the many and various elements of cat behaviour and, as a cat owner myself, I could identify with any owner's (sorry, slave's) pain. The refusal to eat anything but the best brands of food - check. The falling into a deep sleep on the slave's lap at the point the slave is dying for the loo - check. The discovery of dozens of inaccessible (to slaves) hiding places - check. One of my cats used to hide inside the mechanism of a sofa bed and knew there was no way she could be budged! A sweet book for children and adults alike, provided they are happy to have their lives ruled by their cats.'

Lally – Amazon Reviewer

Also by Daniel Riding

The Secret Diary of a Naughty Cat

The Secret Diary of a Naughty Cat: Sunshine Days

Merry Christmas Naughty Cat

The Secret Diary of a Naughty Cat

Daniel Riding

Dedication

To my very own naughty cats,
Raja and Oliver.

Contents

A Note from Naughty Cat:

If you have found this diary and you are a cat, you are welcome to all of my secrets. I hope they help you in your quest to be a naughty cat. If you are a dog and you have found this diary, I don't care what you do with it because dogs are daft and can't read so I could say anything about you and you wouldn't know. Dogs stink,

dogs are dumb, dogs stink...
...oh I already said that. Anyway. If you are a human and you find this diary, I urge you to stop reading now. These secrets of how to be a naughty cat cannot fall into the wrong paws (hands), otherwise our master plan to take over the world is ruined. However if you are a young human and are very good at keeping secrets, then please enjoy this book. I hope you laugh lots and laugh very loudly.

Chapter One

How it all began

Hello folks. Let me introduce myself. My name is… …well, I can't exactly remember because it's been so long since I've heard my own name. You can just call me 'Naughty Cat' because that's what my humans seem to call me all of the time.

Let me tell you though, that's my own doing. It may not be my official name, but I am indeed a naughty cat. I'm also very proud of that fact. I have a lot of fun being 'Naughty Cat'!

Don't get me wrong, my humans love me very much and I love them too. I get fed every day and clean litter all the time so that I have a fresh place to poop (I'm particularly good at super smelly ones, but that's a story for later on).

It's a good life. I sleep when I want, get fussed when I want and pretty much do anything I want, whenever I want. Yes, that does include being very naughty indeed. *Heehee*.

But I want to take you back to the beginning, when I was just a kitten. Before I went to live with my humans. You see I came from a house full of cats, and when I say full, I mean FULL to the top. The lady we all lived with, and by 'we' I mean my many brothers, sisters, aunts, uncles, cousins, distant cousins and… …well, you get the idea. The lady was, shall we say, what most people would call a 'crazy cat lady'.

She always wore brightly coloured clothes that never matched. Her tights were always baggy and her slippers had holes in them because she didn't really walk anywhere. She pretty much just shuffled her feet along the floor like some sort of mad zombie. Her grey hair was crazy, just like she was. When I say crazy, I mean it looked like she'd put her head in the tumble dryer and all the static had made her hair stick out at odd angles, almost like it was trying to run away from her head. I once got too close and had a big whiff of her hair. It wasn't pretty I can tell you. She smelt like old lady, lavender and crusty old hair spray. **Bleurgh!!!!**

Maybe that's why she had no friends, only cats. It could

also be because she spent an awful lot of time shouting odd things at the television. Things like, '*What is she marrying him for?*', '*That dress makes her look like an elephant*', and the one she shouted the most was '*ooooh it's buy one get one free, where's my purse?*' Who wants to have odd things shouted at them? No one! It was only the television that seemed to be able to put up with it. Strange, very strange.

I don't remember much from when I was born. Most kittens don't because they are born with their eyes closed. Don't ask me why, because I haven't got the foggiest idea. It can only be a good thing, because looking back I did not want the first thing I saw to be crazy cat lady's face and her really, really, really hairy chin. Can you just picture it?

Well as you can imagine with so many cats and kittens running around it was difficult to stand out. But not for me, you see I seemed to have an unlimited supply of energy and I put it to good use at every chance I could get. I would often have races around the house with my brothers and sisters and we would dash from room to room as fast as we could. Cheering and whooping as we went, it was so much fun making as much noise as possible. Crazy cat lady didn't seem to mind as she was too busy shouting at the television.

It didn't take long for me to notice that a lot of people came to the house and left with a kitten or two. From what I could hear and see, cat lady was letting people take us to our *new happy homes*. The people that came always seemed nice and very happy to have a new friend to take home. As it turns out, these humans are more than happy to take home a kitten and allow it to grow up and rule over them as their master. I quite liked the idea of having my own humans to look after me and do everything I wished, so I decided to up my game every time a new set of humans visited.

I would act as cute as possible, purring and meowing at whoever popped in. I would run around bouncing everywhere, showing of my athletic skills. I would clean myself all the time to make sure I looked my absolute best. My black fur always shone because I like to be clean and pretty all the time.

Then it happened. A pair of humans stopped by and as I was busy running around, I heard one of them say '*That one*'. It took me a moment to realise they were pointing at me. I looked them over, one was looking very excited and giddy while the other one was smiling even though I knew he had to be the grumpy one of the pair. I was excited, I was getting a new home.

I was picked up and cuddled and it was amazing. The giddy human popped me in a carry case and then they took me to see me new home. I couldn't wait to see the place I would rule over as the master of my new humans.

Chapter Two

Welcome home

Getting home was a little scarier than I thought. As you can imagine I was only used to one home so far, so a change in environment had me just a little nervous. It really didn't take that long to get back to my new home. This was a good thing as I felt very jittery by the time we got there. I remember my humans bringing me inside and placing my carry case on the floor. They unlocked it and opened the door but I didn't move. They peered in at me and tried to coax me out with sweet words and strange kissing noises. This wasn't going to work straight away, I was waiting just a little bit longer to make my move.

Truth be told, I wasn't as nervous as I allowed my humans to believe. This was all part of the master plan, make them see me as being a little scared fluff ball and they would already begin to be under my control. Humans are a sucker for anything cute and fluffy. They offered me food, water and toys but no matter how many jingly things they waggled in my face, I refused to budge. After a while, they decided to potter around doing their own thing. All the while, keeping a nervous and beady eye on me.

Eventually when I was good and ready and had made my humans wait a decent amount of time, I made my move. I crept out of my carry case and decided to go on an adventure exploring my new home. By now my humans were watching me and smiling. I gave a great performance of being a cute and nervous kitty cat, by batting at my new toys and having a quick nibble of my food.

My first goal was to check out my surroundings and work out the best hiding places for me to sneak away to. The first place I found was under the sofa, this is what I call a low-level hiding place. This means while good for hiding, my humans can still quite easily find me. There were a number of hiding places like this, behind curtains and under the coffee table, but these were small-time. I needed to find better places to hide, places that would make my humans nervous when I went missing. Under the bed is a very good hiding place, because even though it is easy for my humans to find me there, if I sit in just the right spot, they're unable to reach me which I find very funny.

Now, I'm going to talk about my mid-level hiding places. These are much better than low-level hiding places, because it takes my humans much longer to find me and they panic a lot more. Because at the time I was a kitten, I found it much easier to squeeze into small spaces and hide away. One of the best places that I like to hide was in the bottom drawer of my human's desk. You see the back of the desk was open against the wall, so I found it very easy to sneak inside the bottom drawer and go to sleep.

You probably already know that most cats like places that are very high up, so it won't surprise you that I love to hide on top of my humans bookcases. I don't know what kind of humans you've met, but my humans don't seem to be particularly clever. They forget to look above them when I go missing. So sometimes I like to crouch down on top of the bookcases and watch them as they get more and more stressed when they can't find me.

I can also be very sneaky when I'm trying to hide. For

example, when my humans are opening drawers and cupboards, whether they are in the kitchen, the bathroom or the bedroom. I'm small enough and fast enough as well as sneaky enough to dart in when they're not looking. *Heehee*.

Sometimes though I get closed in and while this is okay for a very short time, I get very bored. So I meow as loud as I can so that my humans are forced to come and find me and let me out. This also introduced a new nickname that is used only now and again, and that's 'silly cat'. But little do they know that my actions are deliberate, and that my humans are in fact the ones who are silly. Very silly indeed.

High-level hiding places are the ones that should be used sparingly. Because when hiding in these places, it causes my humans to go into such a state of panic that I'm unable to keep these places a secret because I'm giggling too much.

These kind of hiding places are few in number but my absolute favourite place to hide is under the floorboards. You see, in the humans bathroom there's a gap which allows me to slip under the bath and then another gap allowed me to slip under the floorboards.

There is no need to worry, although I don't tell my humans that. Because there is nowhere else I can really go once under the floorboards, it's just a nice secret little space. This kind of hiding place is brilliant for when I'm due to go to the vets. When I'm hiding in this place, I simply refuse all of my human's attempts to lure me out. While this is a very effective hiding place, I have only managed to get my humans to cancel one of my past vets appointments. I really need to work on this, as I really don't like going to the vets.

I am grown up now, and I'm still able to use most of these hiding places. However, some of the smaller hiding places can be a bit of a struggle, so I either don't bother with them or get by bum stuck trying to get in them. Meow.

Chapter Three

I sleep when I want, where I want

Did you know that we cats sleep between 12 to 16 hours a day? You didn't? Well you do now. But I know what you're thinking, "*how can you possibly be so naughty when you have so little time to do it in?*" Well let me tell you it is pretty easy.

All it takes is practice. We don't sleep 12 to 16 hours in one go, we do in small little chunks. It will be an hour here, or a couple of hours there, it's very effective. Plus as a cat I have the choice of when and where I can sleep. I mean, let's face it, as we all know I can do pretty much whatever I want. Don't you wish you could be a cat? If I wasn't a cat, I would wish I was one for sure.

Anyway, where was I? Oh of course, sleep. You may

remember in the last chapter I spoke about my hiding places. Well these can also double up as sleeping places. Which makes them extra great hiding places because if I am asleep, I don't hear my humans calling for me or looking for me. This is very funny as well, but only when I wake up and I realise what has been going on.

Sleeping in short spaces of time, say an hour to three hours is great because it allows me a nap to rest after some seriously naughty behaviour and then once I wake up I am ready to get naughty again. Where do you think the idea of a 'cat nap' came from?

One place that is great to sleep is on the lap of one of my humans. For some reason once I am on their lap and comfy or asleep, they don't want to move for fear of waking me up. I find this highly unusual but it works for me. If they do move me off their lap, I meow and shout at them and climb back on. It's a fun game and I sometimes see how many times I can get my human to move me before they give up. I always win.

What's even funnier is when they really need to go to the toilet. One of my humans drinks so many cups of tea that he is always going to the toilet. So I think it is a great game to see how long they can go before they are bursting so much they have to run and go for a wee. I make myself sleepy and look extra cosy so they feel guilty about moving me. Have you ever been bursting for a wee? Now imagine that feeling with a cat asleep on your tummy. Sometimes I will even wriggle around a bit to get comfy because I know this makes them want to wee even more. It is very naughty to do this I know, but it is so very VERY funny.

One thing that is super naughty but takes very little effort is going to sleep on something you know your humans will need or are currently using. Newspapers, books and magazines are a great start but this only work best if your human is currently reading one of them. No matter where they are reading, I always find a way to climb on top of their book or whatever and somehow I go to sleep instantly. Funny right? My humans don't think so.

I also love to fall asleep on clean clothing that I know they have specifically chosen to wear that day. Not only is clean clothing super comfy and cosy, but it annoys my humans so much because it creases the clothes, covers them in cat hair and means they have to find something else to wear. This is especially funny in the mornings when they are running late for work with toast hanging out their mouth, a cup of coffee in one hand looking like some kind of half-dressed zombie. It's even funnier if they aren't awake enough to realise they have gone to work covered in cat hair. They look super funny running out the door all sleepy and hairy.

Humans are different to us cats in how they like to sleep. They usually sleep in one place which is their bed, and they usually sleep at night for a long time. I counted once and it's usually around 8 to 10 hours. I find this boring because as you know I need attention all the time. So when they are sleeping I like to wait until they are fully asleep, and then dart around from room to room really fast singing the song of my people. And by that I mean meowing really loud, not only is it a lot of fun it is also very annoying for my humans.

Sometimes I go to the furthest place away from the bedroom, so I can get a good run up. I wiggle my bottom, and then charge through every room until I come to the bedroom. Then just as I approach I take a great leap and land with a big thud. My humans wake up in a panic because I have scared them awake. They look at me in shock, and I meow at them and then carry on running around like a crazy cat.

I sometimes love to practice my diving skills. You wouldn't think that a cat would be good at this kind of thing but my diving skills are excellent. For other cats who are not aware of this particular skill let me tell you how it's done. It's best done in the middle of the night when your humans are fast asleep. Find the highest point in their bedroom if you can, I highly recommend the top of a wardrobe or a cupboard. Then mark your target by working out where you will land. The centre of the bed is good, or your humans' stomach is even funnier. Give yourself a good bum wiggle and then leap onto the bed.

Trust me when I say this is ridiculously funny. Your humans may not think so but I find it highly amusing every single time.

This sort of thing can't be done all the time though, so save it for very occasional use. Say when your humans are very tired and grumpy. That is when you get the funniest reaction, and you will find it absolutely hilarious.

Although sometimes I do like being nice, and can always find my way under the bed covers to cuddle up with my humans. I can be slightly less naughty sometimes, but only sometimes.

Chapter Four

Fill My Belly

I absolutely love food. I mean, what cat doesn't? In my opinion feeding time should be all the time and not just when my humans decide.

You see I do have dry biscuits available all the time, which is great but it wasn't always. It didn't take my humans long to discover that, like all cats I am very fussy and have very high standards when it comes to food. Well, when it comes to everything really. Just because I am a cat doesn't mean I can't tell when they have bought me cheap and nasty food. I can taste the difference you know. How do I get around this? I simple refuse to eat what I don't like. To make my point more clear, I will shout as loudly as possible and rub myself against their legs until I get what I want. It works, every single time. I have trained them now to the point where they don't even risk buying me cheap and nasty biscuits, because it is a waste of money.

Also my biscuits have to be full all of the time. Every hour of every day. If there is even the slightest hint of the bottom of my food bowl I will shout as if I am about to starve to make sure they fill it up for me. The key here is to be as dramatic as possible, make such a fuss that your humans have to attend to you immediately. It also acts as a wonderful reminder that you are their top priority. I know how I like things, and we all know that our humans are there to serve us feline royalty. It's just the way things are meant to be.

Now it comes to what my humans call 'wet food'. This is the stuff that comes in a packet and is the most amazing thing I have ever tasted. Imagine what your favourite food is, your absolute favourite and think about how it makes you feel when you eat it. Well when I get wet food it is just like that only so much more amazing.

Again this has to be an expensive type of food, because I simply won't eat the cheap and nasty stuff. My humans once bought a whole big box of different flavoured packets of the cheap cat food because they thought it would last. Well truth be told it did last because I simple refused to eat it. It was horrible. So I point blank refused. They now know just how high my standards are and I eat only the best. Which is exactly how it should be.

However, I have not managed to get my humans to give me wet food every night, but I am still working on this. I can get it most nights, but if I beg for it too often they tell me no, and that I will get fat.

But I wasn't sure what this word 'fat' meant at first, but I soon learnt it means you get bigger and bigger by eating lots and lots of food. I can understand why that would be bad for humans but for us cats it sounds like one the most wonderful things in the world. Being a fat cat actually sounds like a lot of fun. Humans confuse me so much sometimes.

I can however hear the opening of a packet of cat food from miles away, no matter how quiet my humans try to be. I will dash to the kitchen as fast as I can in order to get my mouth around the food I so rightly deserve.

I do also have snacks, little nibbles that are super yummy and are considered occasional treats. I hate that word 'occasional' I would prefer it to be 'all the time' but again this is something I am still working on with my humans. They are quick learners with most of my rules, but other things seems to take them longer to learn. It is quite clear how daft humans are and how more intelligent us cats are in comparison.

I have also worked out that acting super cute and lovable is a great way to get treats. As it turns out, being cute gets me treats. It really is amazing how easily entertained humans can be. I really can't imagine ever being as daft as they are.

Chapter Five

The Gift of the Stink

Can you guess by the title of this chapter what this diary entry will be? It's really easy. We all do it. It is POOP!

Yes, that's right I am talking about that smelly thing we all do that some of us find very funny. Even the word is funny. Poop. POOP POOP POOOOOOOOOP!

As a cat, our humans clean up our poop all the time. Now I know humans do that for their mini humans but that is only when they are very young mini humans. You are then, of course, expected to take care of things yourself. Humans do this for us cats forever. Yes I really do mean forever. Some cats go outside and do their pooping but I know that most cats have what we call a litter box in our homes. It's kind of a box where we do all our pooping. When it gets a certain number of poos in it, our humans will come along and clean it. Not that they enjoy doing this of course. It is just one of the many things they do for us felines as our human slaves. My humans in particular pull some very funny faces when they have to clean up my litter box.

I have been able to perfect the skill of doing really super

smelly ones. You see I may be a small cat but I am very good at make a big bad smell. Sometimes I take the entire day to brew one just so that it will be big and smelly and if I can do that, it can turn my humans faces green.

When I was a kitten, I was super naughty when it came to pooping. Even though I was what humans call 'litter trained', basically I know to go in my litter box, I still found it great fun to poop in secret places and see how long it took my humans to find them, to see how long it took them to 'sniff' them out. *Heehee*.

One of my favourite places to do this when I was a kitten was behind the television. You see it wasn't a place my humans looked behind very often unless it was to find one of my lost toys or something. But if they got a whiff of a super stinky poop I had done, it was really funny to watch them get very stressed trying to work out where I had pooped. The smell was so great that it could fill a room, which meant it was so much harder for my humans to hunt it out and find my poop. This always made for great entertainment.

Another good place I would recommend for giggles, is in the humans bath tub. We cats don't have such things as we can keep clean wherever. But when your human is tired after a very long and very stressful day at work, they look forward to sinking into a nice hot bubble to wash away the stress of the day. So while thinking about this as they head to the bathroom they are already getting excited about this. But I find it highly amusing to ruin this, so what I do is make sure I take a great being steaming smelly dump in the bath. It's so funny watching how their excitement changes very quickly to disgust as they have to clean it out.

I don't do this anymore as a grown up cat because if I still did this then my humans would think there was something wrong with me and they would take me to the vets, which is something no cat enjoys. So now that I am big cat, I have to poop in the proper place. But I still find ways to be naughty and annoying as well.

I love to watch my humans when they take a poop as well. Well not them actually doing one, but I love to watch how embarrassed they get when I wander into the bathroom and simple sit there and stare at them. It is highly inappropriate behaviour as you can imagine but it is really funny. My humans think it is because I don't like being left alone but really I like making them feel awkward and embarrassed.

One thing I do like to do now is time my pooping. Time it perfectly for when my humans are meant to be doing something relaxing.

For example coming home from work. I now have a fairly good idea of when my humans come home from work so I make sure that I go and do a big smelly poop in my litter box just as they are about to come home. So when they come in the front door, they have the wonderful greeting of the smell of my dirty dump. This is super funny, because they pull some really daft faces.

The humans bedtime is also a good time to do this, and

I mean just as they get into bed and get comfy. Because the litter box isn't too far from the bedroom, if I time it right a good stinky poop will waft into the bedroom and make my humans make some really silly noises as the stink hits their noses.

What can I say, but there is a lot to be said for the power of my poop.

Chapter Six

Playtime, Playtime, Playtime

When I was a kitten, playtime was the best thing in the world (after feeding time and pooping time of course!). I had so much energy that I could play for hours and hours. My humans are brilliant when it comes to this, they buy me so many toys it's amazing. I've got bouncy things, squeaky things, cuddly things, shaky things and things to scratch. I have so many toys that I could open my own kitty toy shop. Not that I would bother because I don't share my toys. Humans do, but cats just don't feel the need.

One thing that my humans find annoying is that as a cat I have an obsession with paper in its many different forms. Show me a box of toys and a bit a scrunched up paper and guess which one I choose to play with. That's right, the paper. Scrunch up a bit of paper and throw it and I can bat it around the floor for hours on end. Sometimes though, it can slide and slip under the TV unit and my humans will have to scrunch up another bit if paper for me. Despite how smart I am, and how smart all cats are, we do love a bit of paper. It really can be the simple things in life that keep us entertained.

I love to scratch things. Scratching is so much fun and very good for relieving stress and keeping my claws sharp. I used to scratch chairs, carpets and my humans, but that was apparently not the right thing to do. So my humans decided to spend more money on me and by me a super tall climbing frame with scratching posts included. This has to be the best thing ever. I love to scratch, as well as get up high and I love jumping off great heights onto my humans. This is great fun.

Also what amazes my humans is that I don't let them throw away the box my scratching frame came in. I love boxes. It is just another form of paper after all, and boxes are great for hiding in. I have to be careful though, sometimes I can get too excited over a cardboard box. Last time I got that excited I ended up weeing in the box and it had to get thrown out because it stank.

Oops. I learned my lesson that time. So no more weeing in cardboard boxes when I get them and I can keep them for as long as I can until I destroy them.

You know of course how daft my humans are and how they are nowhere near as clever as I am. They can however do something that must be magic. I have no idea how they do it, so it absolutely must be magic. They can just summon the magic red dot for me to chase around the room. Sometimes it just appears and I can't help myself but chase it all over the place. It's quite an amazing magic red dot because it can go anywhere, even places I can't reach or climb. It can go up the walls and on the ceiling. It can disappear and reappear in a new place on the other side of the room. I just have to chase it wherever it goes. Sometimes my humans can make it go round me in a circle really fast and I chase it so it makes me go very dizzy. So dizzy in fact that when I try to walk, I walk to the side like a crab and then fall over. It's great fun, and it makes my humans laugh until they cry. I have no idea why, as I have already said, humans are daft and strange.

One of the funniest things to play with is toes. Yes you did read that right, I love toes. When my humans walk around the home barefoot, toes are just so tempting to pounce on and attack. They are just so small and wiggly and if I am fast enough I can even give them a good bite. The noises my humans make when I do this are so funny, I almost lose focus when I'm trying to bite them again because I am giggling so much.

I am such a naughty cat, but it is how I make my fun. Naughty, naughty, naughty.

Chapter Seven

It's all about ME

Cats are the most important creatures in the world, but I know I don't need to tell you that dear reader. If you're reading this then you must have some intelligence. You may know (or you may not), that cats have been worshipped since the Egyptian times. The Egyptians would worship us cats as gods and I think that's a wonderful thing and exactly as things should be. In today's world, humans do still worship us but with all their distractions they do need reminding how important we actually are.

You see humans walking around looking at nothing but their mobile phones as if we cats don't exist. This is very frustrating. The best way to get their attention when they are walking about is to parade around and rub up against their legs. It is very effective, and if your human falls over then you can consider it a job very well done.

It is clearly important that I get as much attention as possible, because let's face it, I am the most important thing in my humans lives. If they are not paying me attention then how can they ever really be happy?

I find it best to always make my presence known in the most destructive of ways. Sometimes my humans will be sat staring at the TV like square eyed zombies, so it is my duty to jump in front of the TV show they are watching and shout as loud as possible. I hate to admit that this isn't as effective as I would hope because they just pause the program and pick me up and plop me up on the floor. I find if you do this a number of times they will eventually plop you on the couch with them and fuss you while they mindlessly watch whatever TV show they are currently obsessed with.

What I think many cats need to be aware of is how many things their humans own that are breakable. This may seem extreme but if you want to draw attention to yourself then I suggest pushing a few glasses off tables or pretty much anything you have the strength to push off somewhere high up. It is fun. So much fun that it's a regular trick of mine. I even like to do it slowly while staring at my human, so they know I am not playing games and that it is me who clearly rules the home. It's very hard not to keep a straight face though while I am doing this because the humans panic and shout you see. It's so very funny, watching them clean up something you have smashed only for them to stand up, look at you and realise you are about to do it again with something else.

Another great tip from me is that if your human is paying attention to anything other than you, all you have to do is sit on it. Are they reading a book? Sit on it. Reading a newspaper or magazine? The same thing applies. Just sit on it. Is your human spending hours on their computer typing away on their keyboard? Don't just sit on it, lie across it and stretch out as much as possible. This is a brilliant and effective way to get the attention you deserve.

One thing I did that got some major attention as a kitten was ripping off wallpaper from the walls. As you can imagine this is a super naughty thing you can do so it is best to do this only a couple of times because not only does it get you lots of attention, it also gets you a bit of a telling off which is not a lot of fun.

So when it comes to attention seeking, you do have to be really clever about it and pick your moments. Doing too much of one thing is likely to get you shouted at, and that is not the kind of attention you want.

A nice way of getting attention is just to be really cute and loving. Jump on your humans lap and purr and give them kisses. I may be a naughty cat but I know how to be good on occasion and give lots of love and cuddles. But this can get boring very quickly, so it's back to running around like a mad cat and back to being naughty.

Chapter Eight

Naughty Cat, Naughty Cat, what have you learned?

Well this is the last entry in my first ever diary and I hoped you enjoyed learning all about how a cat can become great at being super naughty.

We have learned about bedtime, feeding time, pooping time and so much more. But these are things that are limited to the inside of your own home.

I wonder what would happen if I could take my naughtiness out into the big wide world. Just what kind of adventures could I get up to, and just how many different and new naughty things can I learn how to do? I bet there are so many more naughty things I can do that I haven't even thought of yet. I need to get my thinking cap on for sure.

Naughtiness is what I do, and it just so happens that I'm very good at it. So good in fact that my humans still love me very much, regardless of how much I like to wind them up and stress them out.

I think I should keep a diary of every single one of my adventures, I am a very interesting and entertaining cat after all. It would be a big shame to not share my amazingness with the world, don't you think? Maybe you should keep an eye out for my next diary, trust me it will be a lot of fun.

But anyway I shall say goodbye for now as my human has just gone to the bathroom and I must go and stare to make him feel silly and uncomfortable.

Goodbye for now,

Naughty Cat

xxx

Acknowledgements

Firstly I would like to thank my Husband for your never-ending love, support and of course, tolerance.

I would like to thank ALL the Authors, writers and bloggers who have supported me over the years. Without your kindness and enthusiasm for my work, this book would never have come into fruition. The online book community is wonderful, and I have made many wonderful friends.

I must say thank you to my two Cats, Raja and Oliver. Not only do they give me an endless supply of writerly inspiration, they make life easier in general.

A Note from the Author

Thank you so much for purchasing and reading my debut Children's book, you don't know how much it means to me that you chose to join me on my adventures with Naughty Cat.

If you have the time it would be wonderful if you popped a quick review for me on Amazon. Not only is it wonderful to hear what you think about my book, your reviews on Amazon help me move up the rankings and get seen by more potential readers.

If you want more information about me and my books then you can find me on social media.

Facebook:
https://www.facebook.com/danielridingwriter

Twitter: https://twitter.com/danielriding

Instagram:
https://www.instagram.com/danielriding

Thank you again, my wonderful readers and keep an eye out for more exciting adventures from Naughty Cat.

Printed in Great Britain
by Amazon